Lin

Weekly Reader Children's Book Club presents

Boris *and the* Monsters

ELAINE MACMANN WILLOUGHBY

Illustrated by Lynn Munsinger

Houghton Mifflin Company Boston 1980

This book is a presentation of
Weekly Reader Children's Book Club.

Weekly Reader Children's Book Club
offers book clubs for children from
preschool through junior high school.
All quality hardcover books are selected by
a distinguished Weekly Reader Selection board.

For further information write to:
Weekly Reader Children's Book Club
1250 Fairwood Avenue
Columbus, Ohio 43216

Library of Congress Cataloging in Publication Data

Willoughby, Elaine Macmann.
Boris and the monsters.

SUMMARY: A young boy fears the monsters of the night until his new watchdog needs his protection.
[1. Night – Fiction. 2. Dogs – Fiction]
I. Munsinger, Lynn. II. Title.
PZ7.W6837Bo [E] 79-22603
ISBN 0-395-29067-8

To Boris, of St. John's Wood

Boris lived on an ordinary street in an ordinary town. Some of the houses were painted bright colors. They were not gloomy at all!

"It's not the sort of place you probably would ever find a monster," said Boris as he sat in the sun on his doorstep. And that's what he said when he sat in the sun.

But when he was in his bedroom in the dark at night it was another matter entirely!

"It's getting dark," said Boris as he watched the street lights turn on and the pink house across the street change from gray to a black box with yellow squares.

"Yes," said his mother. "And it is time for you to go to bed."

Boris shivered a little when he thought about going to bed.

"Do you think there ever could be a monster in my bedroom?" he asked his mother.

His mother smiled. "I have never heard of a monster in any bedroom, have you?"

"No — " said Boris uncertainly. And suddenly he could think of more things that had to be done. Anything to avoid going to bed!

"I just have to feed my goldfish."

Or —

"I just have to work on my airplane."

Or —

"I just have to — "

"The fact is," said his father, "you just have to go to bed!"

After Boris had brushed his teeth and had a story or two he slid under the covers. His father turned out the lights.

"Good night, Boris," said his father.

"Good night," said Boris.

Boris was all alone.

His father started downstairs.

"GOOD NIGHT!" Boris cried loudly.

"Good night," said his father.

"THERE AREN'T ANY MONSTERS HERE, ARE THERE?" he called after his father.

"No," said his father. "There aren't any monsters here at all!"

Boris felt better — for a while. But soon he began to feel that he was not alone. The feeling was mostly in his stomach and it was not a nice feeling. Then he heard a squeak and several groans and suddenly he sat bolt upright in bed!

Boris could see that the dark in his bedroom had become shapes. The shapes seemed to be dancing.

The more he looked the more certain he was that the shapes were monsters. They were big, these monsters, and they had horrible long teeth. Boris's heart beat very fast. He shut his eyes as tightly as he could but he was sure the monsters were getting closer.

He tried to shout "There are no monsters," but it was only a whisper. He slid down under the covers and waited for the monsters to grab him. But he was in luck because they didn't grab him that night!

The next morning Boris was awakened by the sunlight in his room. He got up and looked behind the bookcase and under the bed. He even took a chair and sat in his closet with the light off

for a while. But it wasn't the same in the daylight. "It's all very silly," he said to himself. "THERE ARE NO MONSTERS!" He shouted again to convince himself. "THERE ARE NO MONSTERS!! DO YOU HEAR???"

But that night when the street lights were turned on it was the same thing all over again. And Boris could think of more things that had to be done, to avoid going to bed!

"I just have to pump up my football."

"Do it tomorrow," said his mother. "There are no monsters."

So Boris went to bed. But it was the same. The little noises came. And the monsters came. He slid down under the covers and waited for them to grab him. But he was in luck again because they didn't grab him that night either!

"I just have to finish this picture," Boris said the next night.

"These monsters," said his father, "how do they get into your room?"

"I'm not sure," said Boris, "whether they come in after I get into bed or whether they are already there."

"Well, let's find out," said his father. So together they searched the bedroom — behind the bookcase, in the closet, and especially under the bed. "No monsters here," said his father.

"No," said Boris, "not now there aren't any, but — "

"But you're not certain, are you?" asked his father.

"No," sighed Boris.

"Well," said his father, "I think I would like to meet these monsters." Together the two of them listened for the monster noises. The floor boards snapped and creaked but that's all they heard and they didn't SEE a thing. Soon Boris drifted off to sleep.

The next morning Boris had an idea. "What I need," he said, "is something fierce. Something that would frighten the monsters away."

"Like what?" asked his mother.

Boris thought. "Like a tiger," he said.

"Tigers are fierce, all right," said his father, "but they do not make good house pets. Try something else."

"How about a dog?" asked Boris. "A big, fierce dog!"

"That's a good idea," said his father. So Boris and his father went down to the pet store.

"We want a dog," said Boris.

The man showed them a little poodle.

"No," said Boris, "it has to be bigger and VERY FIERCE!"

"Oh," said the man. "A watchdog."

"Yes," said Boris. "A watchdog!"

"How about this one? He'll grow big and strong and can be very fierce!"

Boris looked at the puppy. "Are you sure he will grow?"

"Positive," said the man.

"I will name him Ivan — Ivan the Terrible," said Boris. "Now I'll feel safe since Ivan the Terrible will keep away the monsters. He even looks fierce now!"

His father agreed. So they paid for Ivan the Terrible and took him home. Ivan growled a little. It wasn't much of a growl, but for a little dog it was a start.

PET SHOP
DOG

That afternoon Boris introduced Ivan the Terrible to some of his friends. "This is my watchdog," Boris explained.

"He is very little for a watchdog," said one.

"He is little now," said Boris, "but he is growing very fast!"

Ivan the Terrible growled another little growl.

Later on the mailman came by and said, "What is that?"
"That is my watchdog," said Boris.
"Well, he isn't very big," said the mailman.
"No, he isn't now," said Boris, "but he will be big some day."
Ivan the Terrible growled and showed his teeth a little.

That night Boris didn't look behind the bookcases or in his closet — and he only looked once under his bed! "All I need is Ivan the Terrible," he said. He put a soft rug on the floor beside his bed for Ivan.

"I'll leave on the hall light," said his mother.

"No," said Boris. "I do not need a light with Ivan the Terrible. Besides," he said firmly, "THERE ARE NO MONSTERS IN THIS HOUSE!" So he got into bed and Ivan the Terrible lay down on the floor near where the monsters came.

But no sooner had his mother and father gotten downstairs than they heard noises — loud noises — mournful, howling noises! They rushed upstairs and in to see Boris. But there was only a lump in his bed. And there was a mournful, howling sound coming from under the covers.

"I'm under here," said a voice. They looked under the blanket and there was Boris. He had his arms around Ivan the Terrible. And Ivan the Terrible was trembling!

"Whatever is the matter?" asked his mother and father.

"Ivan the Terrible is afraid of the dark!" Boris said. "He is so afraid that I am protecting him. Imagine a big, strong, growing dog afraid of the dark."

"Yes," said his father.

"Yes," said Boris. "So I shall just have to protect him until he isn't afraid of the dark anymore! Like me."